So Kestrel, Owl and Whistler the heron flew far and wide to bring back scraps of food for everyone. The larger animals raided dustbins. Fox even persuaded the Stag to bring them some hay, left by the park Warden for the deer to eat.

'It was worth coming to the Park, after all,' said Hare, munching on a carrot.

'And here, humans will never bother us again,' chipped in Mole. 'We're safe in the wildlife sanctuary as long as we can find food.'

Owl circled above the Warden's cottage as she saw the Warden being taken away! He looked very ill. Some men were carrying him into a white van, and then they drove off!

Owl flew to Fox and Badger as fast as she could with the news.

Badger groaned. 'Now we have no protector!'

'The Warden's gone! The Warden's gone!' chattered the squirrels.

'What shall we do?' squealed the rabbits.

'Carry on as normal!' ordered Fox. 'The Park is still a wildlife sanctuary. The danger we face now is the cold of this winter, and starvation.'

And so the animals went off through the snow-covered Park to search for more food.

THE ANIMALS OF FARTHING WOOD
Deer in Danger

Colin Dann

Adapted by Clare Dannatt
Illustrated by Gary Rees
Licensed by BBC Enterprises Ltd

RED FOX

It was winter in White Deer Park. The animals of Farthing Wood couldn't find enough to eat. That happy day when they had been welcomed by the great white Stag seemed a long, long time ago.

'We might as well have stayed in Farthing Wood and let the humans destroy us, if we're going to starve here,' moaned Hare.

'If we help each other, we'll survive,' said Badger. 'Have we forgotten the Oath of Mutual Protection?'

A few days later, the Farthing Wood animals were sharing their scraps of food when a terrifying noise boomed across the Park.

'Gunshot!' gasped Whistler.

Through the darkness of the Park, the shadowy forms of two men crept away from the herd of white deer who were standing frozen in terror. The men were dragging a doe behind them. They had shot her.

'Poachers have come to the Park!' cried Vixen. 'It isn't a sanctuary any more.'

'What can we do about it?' asked Mole helplessly.

'They're after the white deer, anyway - not us,' screeched Weasel.

'But they shared their hay with us,' piped up the mice.

'And made us so welcome here,' said Badger.

'We must do something,' said Fox firmly. 'Every one of us! We shall set up a watch to warn the herd if the poachers come back.'

Owl flew slowly round and round the park boundary. Kestrel and Whistler glided over the woods. Badger moved quietly along the edge of the great stone circle where the deer herd liked to gather. His eyes were trained on them huddling nervously together. Fox and Vixen slipped through the long grass, further away.

Suddenly Vixen froze. 'Keep still,' she hissed. A man's shadow loomed over them - and then was gone.

'There's no time to lose,' said Fox. 'I must warn Stag!'

Little did the poachers know, as they crept stealthily up to the herd, that Fox was also making his way towards the deer . . .

The figure of a man stood up against the sky. Slowly he raised his shotgun until it was pointing directly at the great white Stag. His finger was on the trigger, ready to shoot – when a fierce cry rang through the night.

Fox! His call warned the deer. As Stag bellowed, the deer herd
galloped away.

The poachers aimed wildly after them, and a burst of shots
rang out – and another deer fell to the ground. The poachers
had killed again!

The animal watchers had saved most of the deer that time, but Fox knew that the poachers would come back again. Somehow the animals would have to get rid of the poachers if they were to be safe again.

Day and night the animals watched and waited for the return of the men. And as they watched, they saw the icicles begin to drip and the snow start to melt. The herd of deer moved restlessly around the pond where the ice was thawing slowly. It made Fox think of a plan that might work.

It was evening when Hare burst into the Hollow where the
animals had gathered as usual. 'They're coming!' he gasped.
'Poachers!'

'Kee! Kee!' called Kestrel from high above. 'I can see
them!'

Owl flew as fast as she could to Fox's earth. 'They're here!
The poachers! No time to lose!'

Fox ran as fast as the wind, never stopping till he reached Stag and the deer waiting nervously by the pond.

'The poachers are coming!' he gasped. 'I'll lead them away!'

Fox ran and ran and ran. Now he could see the poachers. Fox let out another scream.

The men froze. Then one muttered, 'It's that fox. He scared the deer off last time.'

'Let's get him first then,' suggested another voice.

Fox's heart began to beat even faster. This was what he had been planning! He dashed out in front of the men – they fired wildly at him, but he was too quick for them.

'After that fox!'

The poachers ran noisily through the woods. Back at the pond, the herd could hear the shouts and crashing getting nearer. Then Fox streaked into the clearing – followed by the panting men.

The men paused, seeing the deer. They raised their guns – but Fox ran in front of the herd.

Fox ran through the deer and on to the ice of the pond. The men ran out after him without a second thought.

Fox reached the far bank just in time as a shot rang out. Just behind him there was a terrific cracking sound as the ice broke beneath the men.

'Help! Help!' they shrieked as they fell into the icy water. Nobody came.

But the poachers managed to drag themselves, wet and shivering, from the pond. Luckily for them it was not deep.

The animals had watched happily as the men were beaten by Fox's cunning. But Vixen stayed quiet. Would the poachers return again – and get their revenge on Fox?

But the men didn't come back and with Spring on its way, Fox decided the animals could all find enough food for themselves.

However, Kestrel and Whistler thought it would be a good joke not to pass on the message to Owl.

'Why all this extra food for us?' Badger asked Owl one evening as she dropped a mouse by his sett.

'The Oath, of course,' said Owl, surprised.

'But Fox ended the food pact ages ago,' said Badger.

'No one told me,' hooted Owl angrily. 'And if they can't be bothered – well, I won't be bothered with that Oath any more.' And she flew off, hurt and furious.

As she flew over the Park, Owl spied two human figures slipping in from outside. She decided not to report what she saw to Fox.

'I'm obviously not taken notice of anyway,' she thought bitterly. 'Let them find out for themselves!'

At the other end of the Park lived a tribe of blue foxes. And as Owl flew on, a young blue fox was wandering in the woods below. He didn't see the human figures creeping silently towards him through the trees, seeking their revenge on Fox – and never knew what hit him.

Owl heard the gunshot and then felt fearful and guilty as she saw the body of a fox in the distance. It was her fault another animal had been shot – she should have kept the Oath.

Fox paced up and down. 'Why kill a blue fox?' he puzzled. 'It's me they're after – and I'm obviously red!'

'In the darkness, who's to tell the difference?' Vixen pointed out gently.

Fox groaned. 'What have I done? The poachers will shoot every fox in the Park to make sure they get me.'

'What have I done?' wondered Owl, too, as she hid from the other animals. She had heard that a fox had died and thought she had caused the death of their own Farthing Wood Fox!

Above the Park, Kestrel flew over the trees. She spied Owl sitting hunched on a branch. Come to think of it, she hadn't seen her for a long time.

'What's up, Owl?'

'It's my fault,' said Owl in a muffled voice.

'What's your fault?'

'That – that – our leader is – dead!' said Owl breaking out into great hooting sobs.

'But Fox is alive and kicking! ' protested Kestrel. And so Owl learned that a blue fox had been killed. And Kestrel realised how cruel the joke she had played on Owl had been – and how much trouble it had caused.

'Never mind,' said Owl. 'We've sorted out everything now. I'm off to patrol the Park again and I'll warn everyone if I see any danger at all.'

Owl's warning hoots spread the news quickly through the Park.
'The Poachers are back! They're killing all the foxes!'

    The great white Stag thought about what he heard. 'The
Farthing Fox helped us when we were in danger,' he said. 'Now
we must help him.'

    Stag walked slowly through the wood towards Fox's earth.

There, he bent his head and talked to Fox for a long time. The plan Stag had thought of was very risky. But it was a risk that had to be taken if the Park was to be rid of the poachers.

'You stay out of sight and we'll take care of the poachers when they come back,' Stag said to Fox.

'Best of luck,' replied Fox.

Once more, two poachers moved quickly through the open parkland, shielding their eyes from the evening sun. They peered through the trees, looking for the deer herd.

Suddenly they heard a loud bellow. They looked up. Through the dazzle of light, they saw a huge pair of antlers looming over them. Stag bellowed again, and before the men knew what was happening, a whole herd of deer was galloping towards them.

A stampede! The poachers fled before the thundering hooves and pointed antlers. No time to raise a gun now! This time they had to run for their lives.

The next evening, Owl saw a light in the Warden's cottage. He was back! But suddenly, Owl spotted the poachers! They were back again too, and shooting at anything that moved.

'The Warden would stop them,' said Fox. 'I'll try to lead the poachers to him!'

Once more Fox prepared for the chase. The two men soon spotted him, still alive to their surprise, and started to follow him. Fox headed towards the Warden's cottage. The men stopped in their tracks.

'Looks like the Warden's at home,' they whispered. 'Let's go.'

They turned round – only to face a row of antlers! The deer were right behind them. The men dodged sideways – and swarms of wild creatures pushed and bit at their legs! The men ran the other way – and birds flew out of nowhere, attacking their heads.

The Warden rushed out of his cottage, gun in hand, to find out what was happening. The animals watched in excited silence as he raised his gun and shouted, 'Hands on your heads, you two!'

As he marched the poachers away, the Warden glanced back towards the crowd of animals. He rubbed his eyes, then shook his head and smiled.

A RED FOX BOOK
Published by Random House Children's Books
20 Vauxhall Bridge Road, London SW1V 2SA

A division of Random House UK Ltd
London Melbourne Sydney Auckland Johannesburg
and agencies throughout the world

First published by Red Fox 1994
Text and illustrations © Random House UK Ltd 1994

Based on the animation series produced by
Telemagination/La Fabrique for the
BBC/European Broadcasting Union
from the series of books about
The Animals of Farthing Wood by Colin Dann

Printed in Slovenia
by Mladinska Knjiga

Random House UK limited Reg. No. 954009.

ISBN 0 09 937011 5